A Time to Fly!

By: Diann Floyd Boehm
Illustrated by: Nancy Hoover

A Time To Fly!

By: Diann Floyd Boehm
Illustrated by: Nancy Hoover

Published by

Texas Sisters Press, LLC
www.TexasSistersPress.com

©2022 Diann Floyd Boehm

ISBN: 978-1-952041-62-4 (Hardcover)
ISBN: 978-1-952041-63-1 (Paperback)
ISBN: 978-1-952041-64-8 (Ebook)

"Mommy where is everyone?" chirped the little bluebird.

"Your brother and sister are in the tree with Daddy.
I am right here on the rooftop waiting for you to fly
with us," the mommy bird sweetly tweeted back.

"But Mommy, why can't we stay in our warm nest?
I love it here," chirped the baby bird as he hopped back
in the nest where his mommy could not see him.

"I know you do. Would you like to hear a story?
I'll tell you about when you were a little egg.
Then when I say 'flap your wings,' you flap them and
I will continue the story. Okay?" the mommy bird
warmly asked.

"Okay, Mommy," the birdie tweeted. He jumped up and perched on the flowerpot that held the family nest.

"Well, your daddy and I were looking for the perfect place to build a nest. One day we were on a rooftop singing to our friends, and we heard these beautiful chimes.

"We looked down and saw an empty flowerpot hanging by the chimes, so we decided to scout around.

The flowerpot looked warm and cozy. We knew critters would not get our eggs, so we began to build a nest inside the pot."

"We laid three little eggs and watched over them day and night. Now flap your wings one time," tweeted the mommy bird.

The little bird flapped his wings just a tiny bit. "Very good," the mommy bird warmly tweeted.

"Seventeen whole days went by, and we knew you would be born soon, and sure enough, on the 20th day, you and your brother and sister decided to hatch.

Now flap your wings one time," tweeted the mommy bird.

"Oh, that is exciting, Mommy," chirped the little bird as he flapped his wings a little harder.

"Then your brother and sister and you hatched. You were all so tiny, your little eyes were still closed, and you didn't even have your feathers yet.

Now flap your wings one time," tweeted the mommy bird. "We must have been cold," tweeted the little bird as he flapped his wings a bit longer.

"The nest helped keep all of you warm, explained the mommy bird.

"Next, your daddy and I would feed all of you, and we watched you grow. It was exciting, and oh, could all of you eat!

On the 8th day, the three of you opened your eyes. You saw your daddy and me for the first time.

Now flap your wings."

"Wow!" tweeted the bird as he flapped his wings a little higher with delight.

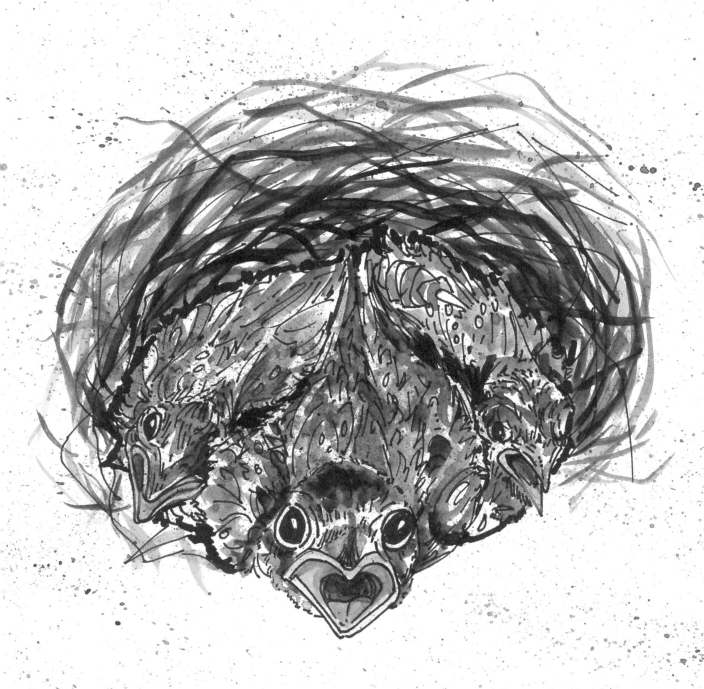

"Well, your feathers were starting to show, and you were eating more worms. Before we knew it, all your feathers had come in."

"I like my feathers!" the little bird tweeted glee.

"Of course, you do."

Now, your daddy and I would watch over all of you. We took turns being in the tree or on the rooftop.

It's time to flap your wings again," the Mommy bird said.

"I like having all my feathers, Mommy," the young bluebird tweeted, as he flapped his wings a tiny bit faster.

"Then one day, your brother took flight and flew to your daddy and me in the tree. We were very excited, but you and your sister were not ready. That was okay. Each one of you flies when you are ready.

Well, the next day, your little sister decided to fly and join her brother.

Now flap your wings," said Mommy bluebird.

"Okay, Mommy, but I'm not scared. I like it right where I am," answered the little bird.

"Of course, you do, but you know what, we will come back and visit. But for now, the weather is changing, and Mommy and Daddy want you to meet the rest of your family," she lovingly explained.

"You mean there are more of us!" the little bird exclaimed.

"Sure, there are, and we all can not fit in the nest.
Why, look at you. You take up the whole nest now!"
the mommy bird tweeted.

"Oh, I do! I did not realize it," the little bird tweeted.

"Okay, little one, I want you to flap your wings two times."
So the little bird started to flap, but lost his balance
and fell into the nest.

"It's okay," tweeted the mommy bird. "Now, come
back out."

The little bird peeked out to see what he could see.
Then he ducked back in his nest.

"Here I am, Mommy," he chirped.

"I see you, dear. Now would you like to see your daddy? He is right over there on the tree.

"Sure, Mommy."

"Okay, when I say start flapping, flap your wings and don't stop. Ready?"

"Ready, Mommy."

"Start flapping, great, keep it up! Flap, flap, flap," Mommy excitedly called out.

The little bird went up and up and soon started to fly. The mommy bird joined him, and he flew to the rest of his family in the tree.

Everyone was so excited. The little bird was so proud of himself.

They flew over by the nest, circled, and went high in the sky. The little bluebird and his family were off to join the others to fly south for the winter.

The little bluebird started to turn around, but his mommy flew next to him and reminded him they would be back next year!

"Okay, Mommy!" As he flew higher in the sky, he tweeted, "I knew I could do it!"

About the Author
Diann Floyd Boehm

Diann is an author, educator, community volunteer, humanitarian, and former classroom teacher. Diann is passionate about storytelling. She is the author of nine books, some for younger children, some for YA and adults.

Her **Little Girl in the Moon** has delighted children all over the world. **The Little Girl in the Moon Series** is now **The Moonling Adventures!** The little boy in the moon and his dog Shadow are introduced in **The Moonling Adventures – The Serengeti**.

The Moonling Adventures – The Serengeti won "Best Texas Children's Book 2021".
Harry the Camel has won two book awards, and was the number one children's bookseller in the B4R store! **A Song of Peace** won honorable mention in the Author Bookfest 2022, and was Story Monster approved for parents by the Story Monster Magazine.

Diann is the cohost of four shows on USA Global TV. She is married, a mother of three, and one grandchild. Diann loves to help young and old to "Embrace Imagination!
You can learn more about Diann at **www.diannfloydboehm.com**

About the Illustrator
Nancy Hoover

Nancy Hoover has had a varied career as an artist, teacher, illustrator, photographer, art gallery director, and muralist. A long-time Austin, TX., resident, her art has appeared in galleries all over the world and was included in the Smithsonian Institute's catalog, Renwick Gallery, Washington, DC. She has received many local and national art awards, including The People's Choice Award from the City of Austin.

Currently the Art Director for The Girls' School of Austin, she has developed the school's nationally recognized art program, with her students winning numerous regional and national accolades. She also has had her projects published in Scholastic ART magazine and has illustrated several books.

Nancy earned a BFA degree from the College of Charleston and did her graduate work in Art at the University of Georgia and the University of Central Florida.

She is married, has 2 adult sons, and looks forward to her grandchildren reading this book!

CPSIA information can be obtained
at www.ICGtesting.com
Printed in the USA
BVHW020724190722
642462BV00011B/8

9 781952 041624